Why is Cory Brown?

written and illustrated by

Michelle Jestice

Priority Publishing Company

Why is Cory Brown?
by Michelle Jestice

Priority Publishing Company
PO Box 1779
Lynn Haven, FL 32444
www.priority-publishing.com

ISBN 978-0-9754749-2-1
ISBN 0-9754749-2-8
Children's Fiction

Printed in the United States of America

To Dylan, Amanda, Grayson, and Sophie

You teach me to ponder differences in others and then to embrace those differences with acceptance and love, instead of fear.

Thanks to Wendy, Scott, Stewart, Susie, Paul, Dr. LeClere, and LaTanja for their eyes, ears, and encouragement.

Thomas sits on the front step and ties his shoes. His mother sits close by in case he needs help. When he finishes he stands and says, "I'm ready. Let's go!"

Each day Thomas and his mother walk to the park. He asks endless questions along the way.

"Mama, why do the birds sing?
Why is the grass green?
Who makes the flowers grow?
Where does the rain go?"

She listens to his many questions, answers
the ones she can and ponders the ones she cannot.

As soon as he sees the playground, Thomas runs to the swings and calls, "Mama, push me high in the sky!"

She pushes him on the swings until he asks to slide.

Climbing to the top he calls, "I'm gonna race down. Catch me!" His mother laughs and scoops him into her arms when he reaches the bottom.

After playing, he and his mother sit on their
favorite, wooden bench next to an old, oak tree at the
edge of a field of wildflowers. Sipping cool water, he
says, "I like the flowers mixed with green grass."
"Yes," she smiles and replies. "They're beautiful."
After enjoying the rest of their water, they begin
to walk home.

On the way home, Thomas sees his friend Cory. Cory rides toward them on a red bicycle squeezing his shiny, silver horn.

Thomas studies Cory's dark eyes and dark hair. He thinks about Cory's brown skin. It looks like chocolate. He wonders what makes Cory's skin different from his own.

"Hi Cory," he calls and waves. "Can you play?"

"I'll ask my mom, but I know she has to run some errands," Cory replies.

They both sigh aloud, knowing that errands are boring and mean that kids cannot play.

Thomas and his mother walk the rest of the way home. She makes lunch while he kneels on the carpet and pushes his cars around an imaginary racetrack.

"Lunch is ready," she calls.

Thomas nibbles his peanut butter sandwich and grapes without talking. Mama knows something is on his mind.

After finishing his lemonade, Thomas runs to the window to see if any kids are playing.

"Do you see anyone?" Mama asks.

"No," he answers, disappointed. "Can we read a book?"

"Sure," she says.

He chooses a book about children from different countries and their homes.

They sit on the sofa reading together. After his mother finishes the book, Thomas looks at her. His eyebrows come together and his head tilts to one side. He asks, "My skin is light, and Cory's skin is dark. Mama, why is Cory brown?"

She raises her eyebrows and ponders for a moment. "Hmmmm. Good question. Let me think about that one, Thomas." The doorbell rings.

Hopping off the couch, he races to answer the door.

"We're home!" announces Cory. "Can you play?"

Thomas looks at his mother. She smiles and nods yes.

They join the other children who are outside. Thomas's mom thinks hard about her answer. After a while, she calls to him, "Thomas, come here please. I want to ask you something."

He and Cory ride their bikes over to her.

Mama asks, "What does your friend Lori look like?"

"She looks nice."

"Right. We usually don't think about her skin and hair. But, what does she look like?"

"Well, she has light skin and bouncy hair," Thomas replies.

"Do you think she looks like her parents?" Mama asks.

"I guess."

"What about Lucas? What does he look like, Cory?"
"He has brown skin, brown eyes, and black hair."
She asks, "Do you think Lucas looks like his parents?"
The boys look at each other, laugh and shrug.

Mama explains, "God makes all kinds of people in the world. Some have dark skin. Some have light skin. Some have red hair. Some have brown hair. Some have blue eyes. Some have brown eyes. We may have different eyes, skin, and hair, but God creates us just as He wants us to be."

Checking out their own skin, both boys look down at their arms. Then, they look at each other with wide eyes and raised eyebrows.

They look at the kids on the sidewalk.

Thomas smiles at his mother, turns toward the sidewalk and yells, "Wait up," to the children riding bikes.

After pedaling to the others, Thomas looks at Jeannie's light skin, blonde hair, and blue eyes. He looks at Brian's light brown hair and freckled skin.

Studying his friends, Thomas thinks about how God makes each of us different.

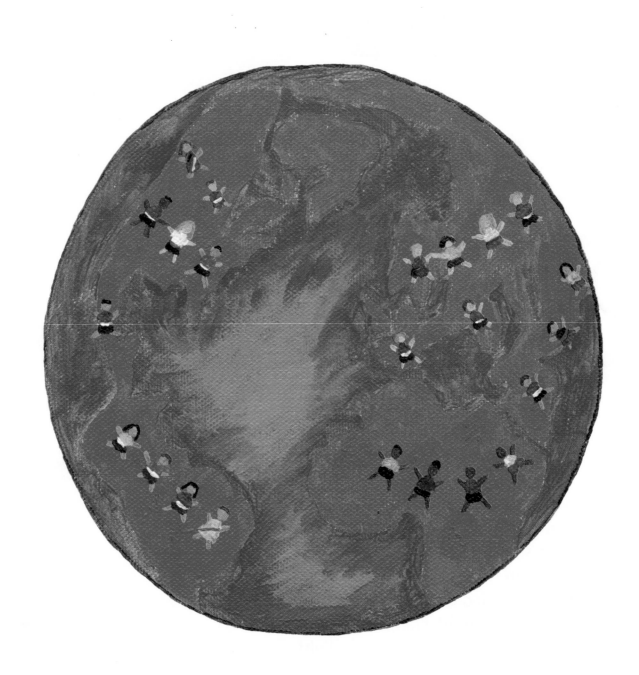

The next day at the park, Thomas slides down the slide a few times.

His mother pushes him on the swing. Then they sit on their favorite bench to sip cool water.

She says, "See the flowers in the field? The reds, oranges, yellows, greens, blues, and purples make each flower special. Yet, it takes all of them together to create the beautiful field we admire every day."

Looking at her, he kicks his feet in the dirt while she talks.

"God makes each flower. God makes each person. It takes many colors and shades of people to create our beautiful world."

With his hands in his pockets, Thomas slowly walks home thinking about the wildflowers. He kicks rocks on the sidewalk and squats to look at bugs.

Later that day Thomas asks Cory to play. He knocks at the door, and Cory's mom answers.

"Hi, Mrs. Johnson, can Cory play?" Thomas asks.

"Sure," she smiles. Peeking around the door, Cory looks to see who is there.

"Hi, Cory," Thomas says. "Do you want to play?"
Squeezing out the door, Cory nods and calls, "I'll race you!"
The boys race to Thomas's house. "Let's build something," Cory says.

"Okay," Thomas agrees and dumps the huge bin of blocks onto the floor. The boys sit and build houses, roads, and buildings out of blocks.

"Let's make the tallest tower in the world," says Cory.

The boys pile one block on top of another.

As they build, Thomas steps back and looks at the red, yellow, green, and blue blocks.

"Cory, look at all the colors in our huge tower."

Cory looks at Thomas with a squinched-up face. "What are you talkin' about?"

Mama listens from the next room.

"Remember? God makes the world with different colors, like you and me," Thomas explains. "God makes brown skin and light skin and dark skin to build the world--like the blocks in our tower."

Cory grins back and says, "You're weird. Let's knock down the blocks and go ride bikes."

"Okay," says Thomas.

Mama watches the boys knock over the tower and put the blocks away. Thomas looks back at her before he runs outside. She smiles at him and says, "I'm so proud of you. You understand perfectly."

He returns the smile and yells, "Cory, wait for me!"

The boys jump on their bikes and ride down the sidewalk.

Watching the boys from the front porch, Mama smiles to herself thinking--I must have the most important job in the world.

We hold these truths to be self-evident,
that all men are created equal,
that they are endowed,
by their Creator,
with certain unalienable Rights,
that among these are
Life, Liberty,
and the pursuit of Happiness.

(from the U.S. Declaration of Independence, 1776)